This book is to be returned on or before
the last date stamped below.

# SONNY'S WONDERFUL
# WELLIES

## Lisa Stubbs

# To MUM

Designed by Rebecca Elgar
Printed and bound in Belgium by Proost
for the publishers Piccadilly Press Ltd.,
5 Castle Road, London NW1 8PR

ISBN: 1 85340 369 5 (hardback)
1 85340 495 0 (paperback)

10 9 8 7 6 5 4

A catalogue record of this book is available from the British Library

Lisa Stubbs lives in Wakefield. She trained in Graphic Communications at Batley Art College and has illustrated greetings cards for a number of years. This is her first book. Her other books, SONNY'S BIRTHDAY PRIZE, SONNY'S TREASURE HUNT and ED AND MR ELEPHANT: THE BIG SURPRISE are also published by Piccadilly Press.

SONNY'S TREASURE HUNT
ISBNs: 1 85340 555 8 (hardback)
1 85340 571 X (paperback)

SONNY'S BIRTHDAY PRIZE
ISBNs: 1 85340 422 5 (hardback)
1 85340 427 6 (paperback)

ED AND MR ELEPHANT:
THE BIG SURPRISE
ISBNs: 1 85340 530 2 (hardback)
1 85340 565 5 (paperback)

# SONNY'S WONDERFUL
# WELLIES

## Lisa Stubbs

PICCADILLY PRESS

When Sonny's grandma gave him
a pair of red wellington boots,
Sonny tried them on immediately.
"They're wonderful," he said.

"Thank you very much!"

Sonny wore his wellingtons
all morning in the house.

When they went shopping
at lunchtime

Sonny hoped
that it would rain.

But it didn't.

Sonny wore
his wellingtons
anyway.

Sonny wore them to tea
at his friend's house.

And he wore them while watching television.

Sonny even wore them to bed.

The next morning, Sonny looked
out of the window.
There wasn't a cloud in the sky.
"Why doesn't it rain?" he said very crossly.
"I want to stomp and splash
in my wonderful wellies."

After playgroup it was sunny.
He walked home with
        big tears in his eyes.

"Never mind," said Grandma.
"I have an idea."

Soon Sonny was stomping
and splashing and having
a lovely time.

When Mum came home she joined
Sonny in the paddling pool.

They had so much fun Sonny said that
he didn't care if it never rained again.

But you'll never guess
what happened . . .